MAILBOX MAGIC

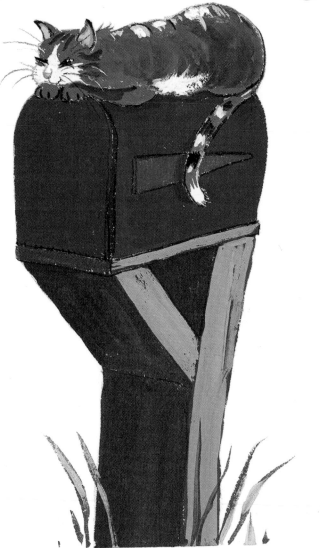

For
Eric
the
Great

Library of Congress Cataloging-in-Publication Data
Poydar, Nancy.
Mailbox magic / Nancy Poydar.—1st ed.
p. cm.
Summary: A young boy who wants to receive mail of his own
sends away for an offer he sees on the back of a cereal box.
ISBN 0-8234-1525-2
[1. Postal service—Fiction. 2. Perseverance—Fiction.]
I. Title.
PZ7.P8846 Mai 2000
[E]—dc21   99-051776

MAILBOX MAGIC

Nancy Poydar

Holiday House / New York

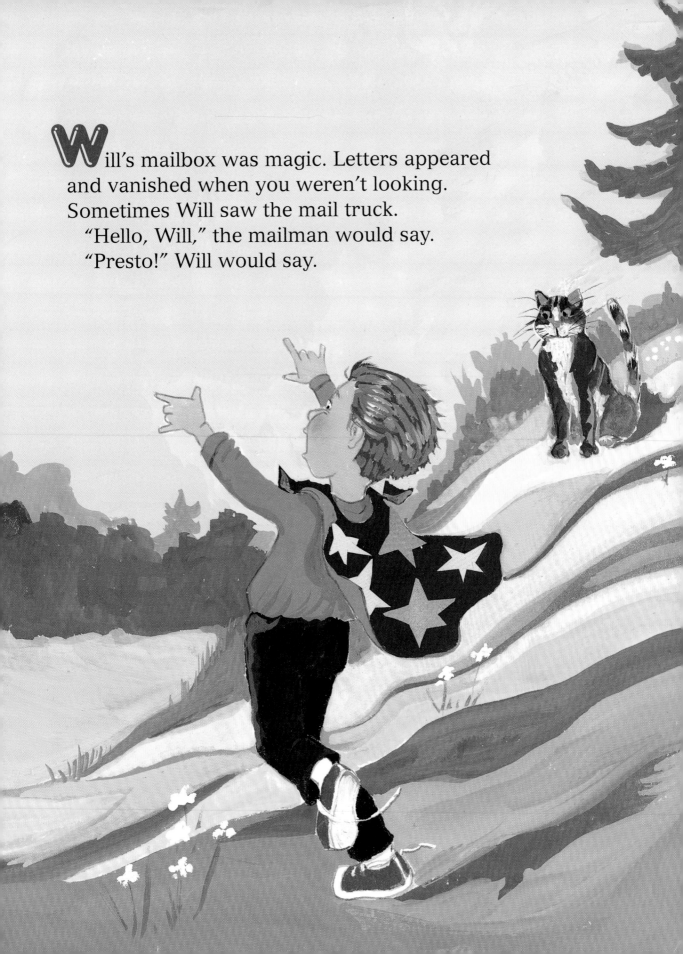

Will's mailbox was magic. Letters appeared and vanished when you weren't looking. Sometimes Will saw the mail truck.

"Hello, Will," the mailman would say.

"Presto!" Will would say.

There were big letters. There were letters with windows.
There were pamphlets with pictures. There were ads. But
none of it said "Will." Will wished and wished that one of
the letters would be for him.

"Someday you'll get mail," his mother said.
"I feel it in my bones."

Will watched his mother write letters.
He wrote,

DEAR WILL,
YOU ARE GREAT!
FROM WILL

He put his letter in an envelope. He put on the
address. He put on the stamp.

"Your letter goes to the post office," his mother said. "Then it gets sorted and sent out. They will say, 'A letter for Will!' and give it to our mailman. He will know which mailbox to put it in."

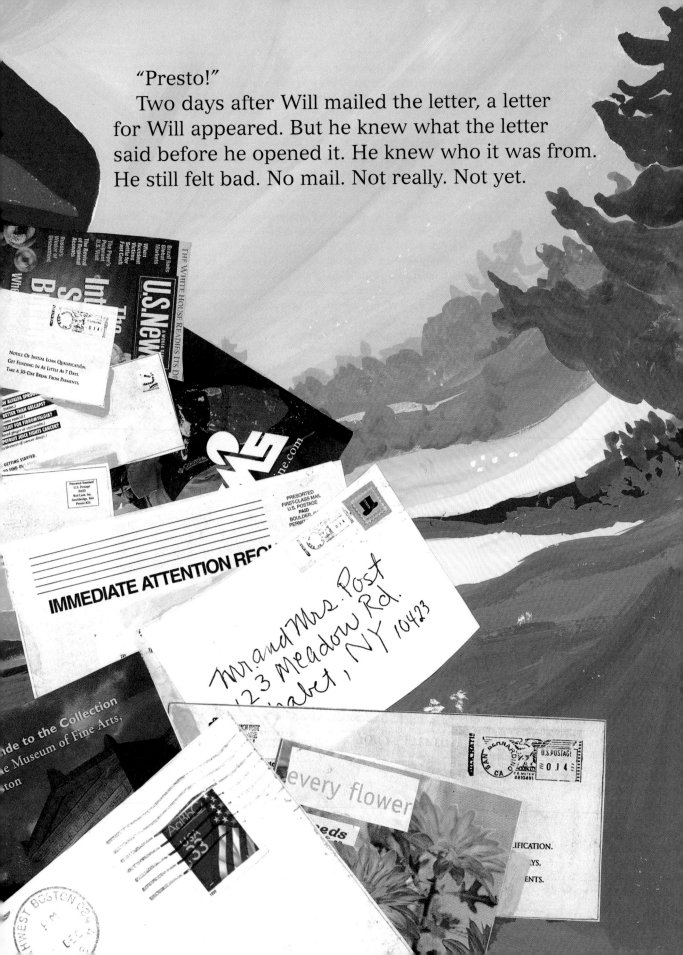

"Presto!"

Two days after Will mailed the letter, a letter for Will appeared. But he knew what the letter said before he opened it. He knew who it was from. He still felt bad. No mail. Not really. Not yet.

One morning, Will saw a picture of a boy and a girl mailing letters. The picture was on a cereal box. The children had each eaten three boxes of Magic Charms and cut out a special label from each.

They were sending away for personalized cereal bowls. Their names would be on the bowls. The picture of the bowl was on the other side of the box. It would come in the mail.

Will ate two bowls of cereal that morning. He fixed one for his father. He fixed one for his mother. "You'll feel good all day!" Will proclaimed. "Magic Charms makes you healthy and strong. You'll feel it in your bones!"

"No," his mother said later. "You can't have cereal for lunch." Will had a bowl of cereal for dessert.

Will brought a bowl of cereal to the mailman.

"Why, thank you, Will," the mailman said. He didn't want a second bowl.

Will invited his friend Jennifer for breakfast. Jennifer had two bowls of Magic Charms; so did Will.

"Wait till you see my personalized cereal bowl," he said to Jennifer. "It's going to say 'W-I-L-L.' It's going to come in the mail."

"Great," Jennifer said.
"Magic," said Will.

It is almost impossible to make
the cereal in three boxes vanish.
But Will did the impossible.

It is tricky to cut the labels off
three boxes. But Will did tricks.

It takes know-how to mail labels to the cereal company. But Will had know-how. He wrote:

```
PLEASE
SEND ME
MY BOWL.
FROM
WILL THE GREAT
```

He put the letter in an envelope. He wrote the address. He put on the stamp.

"Abracadabra!"

Will began to wait right then!

In the sun.

Under the stars.

In the rain.

Letters appeared, but nothing for Will. Not yet.

Will's mother told him the cereal-company people had to send his letter to the bowl factory. The bowl-factory people would make his bowl and send it to him.

"What's taking your package so long?" Jennifer asked.

"Right now they are painting the 'W' at the bowl factory," Will said.

"It must be a big 'W'," she said.

"The best!" said Will. "And the 'I' and the 'L's. They are the greatest letters on earth."

"I guess that's some bowl," said Jennifer.

"The bowl-factory people take the box with my cereal bowl in it to their post office. Their mailman stamps the box and puts it on a mail train. Our post office gets it from the mail train. Our mailman puts it in his truck and brings it to my mailbox."

"Will, a box in your mail!" shouted Jennifer.

It's tough to open boxes that come in the mail.
But Will was tough.

"Presto!"

"That's some bowl!" said Will's father.

"Will, you have know-how," his mother declared.

"Are you going to fill it with Magic Charms?" asked Jennifer.

"Oats," said Will.

"Oats?"

"For when my horse gets hungry."

"Horse?"

"Now I'm going to find a cereal company that sends horses!" Will said. "I feel it in my bones."

MAILBOX KNOW-HOW

Be sure your letter carrier
knows where to deliver
the letters you send:

1. Put your picture or letter
   in an envelope and seal it.

2. Write the name of the person
   you are writing to on the front
   of the envelope.
       Underneath the name,
   write the number and street.
       Underneath the street address,
   write the city or town and the
   state. Write the zip code, too.

3. Now write your name and
   address, including the zip code,
   on the envelope in the upper
   left corner or on the top
   of the back.

4. Stick the stamp in the upper
   right corner on the front.

5. Mail it.
   ABRACADABRA!

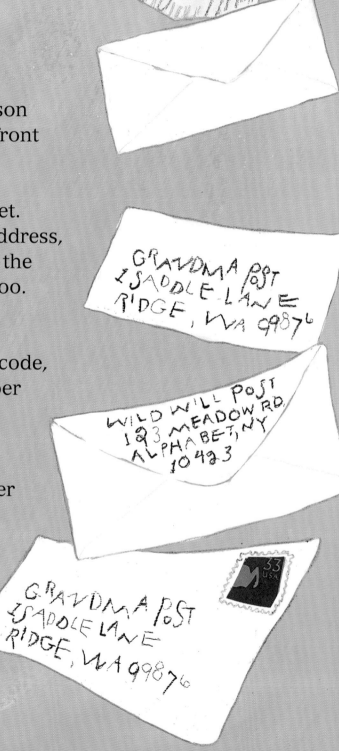